Put Beginning Readers on the Right Track with
ALL ABOARD READING™

The All Aboard Reading series is especially designed for beginning readers. Written by noted authors and illustrated in full color, these are books that children really *want* to read—books to excite their imagination, expand their interests, make them laugh, and support their feelings. With fiction and nonfiction stories that are high interest and curriculum-related, All Aboard Reading books offer something for every young reader. And with four different reading levels, the All Aboard Reading series lets you choose which books are most appropriate for your children and their growing abilities.

Picture Readers
Picture Readers have super-simple texts, with many nouns appearing as rebus pictures. At the end of each book are 24 flash cards—on one side is a rebus picture; on the other side is the written-out word.

Station Stop 1
Station Stop 1 books are best for children who have just begun to read. Simple words and big type make these early reading experiences more comfortable. Picture clues help children to figure out the words on the page. Lots of repetition throughout the text helps children to predict the next word or phrase—an essential step in developing word recognition.

Station Stop 2
Station Stop 2 books are written specifically for children who are reading with help. Short sentences make it easier for early readers to understand what they are reading. Simple plots and simple dialogue help children with reading comprehension.

Station Stop 3
Station Stop 3 books are perfect for children who are reading alone. With longer text and harder words, these books appeal to children who have mastered basic reading skills. More complex stories captivate children who are ready for more challenging books.

In addition to All Aboard Reading books, look for All Aboard Math Readers™ (fiction stories that teach math concepts children are learning in school); All Aboard Science Readers™ (nonfiction books that explore the most fascinating science topics in age-appropriate language); All Aboard Poetry Readers™ (funny, rhyming poems for readers of all levels); and All Aboard Mystery Readers™ (puzzling tales where children piece together evidence with the characters).

All Aboard for happy reading!

To my Maggie, the real Undercover Kid.—R.K.
Dedicated to Secret Agents Zoe, Tori, Mia,
Tyler, Logan and Dan—A.L.S.

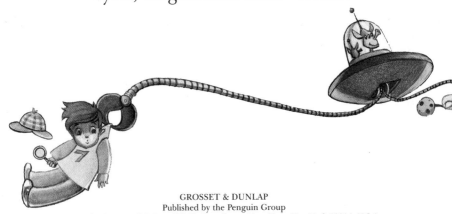

GROSSET & DUNLAP
Published by the Penguin Group
Penguin Group (USA) Inc., 375 Hudson Street, New York, New York 10014, U.S.A.
Penguin Group (Canada), 90 Eglinton Avenue East, Suite 700, Toronto, Ontario, Canada M4P 2Y3
(a division of Pearson Penguin Canada Inc.)
Penguin Books Ltd, 80 Strand, London WC2R 0RL, England
Penguin Ireland, 25 St Stephen's Green, Dublin 2, Ireland
(a division of Penguin Books Ltd)
Penguin Group (Australia), 250 Camberwell Road, Camberwell, Victoria 3124, Australia
(a division of Pearson Australia Group Pty Ltd)
Penguin Books India Pvt Ltd, 11 Community Centre, Panchsheel Park, New Delhi - 110 017, India
Penguin Group (NZ), Cnr Airborne and Rosedale Roads, Albany, Auckland 1310, New Zealand
(a division of Pearson New Zealand Ltd)
Penguin Books (South Africa) (Pty) Ltd, 24 Sturdee Avenue, Rosebank, Johannesburg 2196, South Africa

Penguin Books Ltd, Registered Offices:
80 Strand, London WC2R 0RL, England

Text copyright © 2006 by Ronald Kidd. Illustrations copyright © 2006 by Andy Sklar. All
rights reserved. Published by Grosset & Dunlap, a division of Penguin Young Readers Group,
345 Hudson Street, New York, New York 10014. ALL ABOARD MYSTERY READER and
GROSSET & DUNLAP are trademarks of Penguin Group (USA) Inc. Printed in the U.S.A.

Library of Congress Cataloging-in-Publication Data

Kidd, Ronald.
Undercover Kid : tuna surprise / by Ronald Kidd ; illustrated by Andy Sklar.
p. cm. -- (All aboard mystery reader. Station stop 3)
Summary: When Maggie Murphy's grandfather visits he brings many mysteries, including an
invention that may help eight-year-old Maggie, who loves being a spy, to solve a neighborhood
crime--who is stealing the tuna fish from outside Mr. Kling's shop?
ISBN 0-448-44128-4 (pbk.)
[1. Spies--Fiction. 2. Inventions--Fiction. 3. Family life--Fiction. 4. Mystery and detective stories.] I. Sklar, Andy, ill. II. Title. III. Series.
PZ7.K5315Und 2006
[Fic]--dc22
                2005036314   10 9 8 7 6 5 4 3 2 1

UnderCover Kid

Tuna Surprise

By Ronald Kidd

Illustrated by Andy Sklar

Grosset & Dunlap

Chapter One

A woman yelled. A cat was crying. There was a broken lamp. The tuna fish was gone.

It was a case for the Undercover Kid.

My name is Maggie Murphy. You
probably think I am just a regular person.
That is where you are wrong.

I am a spy.

Spies wear cool clothes. They lurk. What is lurking? I would tell you, but the spy code does not allow me to.

The spy code is a little notebook that I carry in my pocket. It contains all the spy rules, such as:

1. Wear cool clothes.

2. Use sunglasses as much as possible.

3. Talk in a special low voice.

4. Lurk at all times.

5. Do not say what lurking means.

7

I live in a place called the Village. There are no houses. Instead, there are stores. My dad owns one of them. It is a used book store. The store is Papa's Books. My family lives above the bookstore. My family is me, my dad, and my mom. Oh, yeah. There is also Arthur. He is my little brother.

He may not be in my family much longer. I am hoping that aliens take him away.

Arthur is six. I am eight. That means I am in charge. Will you please explain that to him?

There are lots of other stores in the Village. There is Dippin' Donuts. There is Shiny Bright Cleaners. There is a pet store called Fido's.

There is a lamp store. The name of it is the Lighthouse. If you were a spy, you would have noticed that I just gave you a clue.

Lamps, get it? At the start of the story I said there was a broken lamp. That is where the mystery started. At the lamp store.

Chapter Two

I was right outside the store, lurking, when it happened. Suddenly, there was a crash.

I ran inside. Mrs. Levine, the owner, was staring down at the floor. A gray cat stood next to a broken lamp.

My giant spy brain leaped into action. "A cat broke your lamp," I said.

Mrs. Levine picked up the cat. She yelled at it, "How did you get in here?"

Nearby, a small voice said, "You left your back door open."

Arthur stepped out from behind a lamp. I groaned. He stuck his tongue out at me.

Arthur said, "I got in through the back door. Maybe the cat did, too."

Mrs. Levine went to the back door to put out the cat. Just then, a police officer came bursting through the door. He held out his arms.

"Sweetikums!" he said.

"I beg your pardon?" said Mrs. Levine.

"My darling," said the officer, "I was so worried."

He reached for Mrs. Levine. She backed up. He took the cat from her and hugged it.

Get it? Sweetikums wasn't Mrs. Levine. It was the cat.

The man was my friend, Mr. Kling. He owned the costume shop next door, called Only Make Believe.

You never knew what costume Mr. Kling would be wearing. He had been a doctor, a football player, and the queen of Sheba. Today he was dressed as a police officer.

"Where did that cat come from?" asked Mrs. Levine.

Mr. Kling said, "I found her in the alley a few weeks ago. Every morning I have been putting tuna fish on a plate next to my back door for her to eat. Today someone took the tuna fish—and the plate, too."

"That's why the cat came into my store," said Mrs. Levine. "It was looking for food."

I said, "Yes, but who took the tuna fish?"

"That," said Mr. Kling, "is a mystery."

Chapter Three

That night at dinner, all I could think about was tuna fish. My dad had something else on his mind: frogs.

He and the other store owners wanted more people to shop in the Village. So they had made signs that said, "The Village is jumping." There was a picture of a frog on all the signs. Get it?

They had a contest. Every store in the Village got a big cardboard frog to decorate. The store with the best frog would get a prize.

My dad was trying to decide how to decorate our frog. "Maybe we could put my picture on the frog's face," he said.

I tried to imagine my dad's face on a big cardboard frog.

I said, "Keep working on it, Dad."

My mom said, "I have some exciting news. Kids, your grandfather is coming to visit."

"Oh, boy!" said Arthur. "I love Grandpa Murphy!"

My mom said, "It is not Grandpa Murphy. It is your other grandfather."

"What is he like?" Arthur asked.

"He is a very sweet man," said my mom. "But he is a little bit strange."

"How long will he stay?" I asked.

"We don't know," said my mom.

I smiled. "Is this a mystery?"

"I guess you could say that," said my dad.

Chapter Four

Two mysteries in one day! My brain was speeding like a special spy airplane.

I wondered who the tuna fish thief was. I decided to do a special spy search. I started the very next day by lurking in the Village.

As I lurked, I noticed a strange machine driving down the street. The front of it was like a car. The back of it was like a van. It sputtered and groaned. Clouds of smoke poured out.

I hurried after the car. It was not easy. It is hard to hurry and lurk at the same time.

The car slowed down and parked. A man got out. He was wearing overalls, tennis shoes, glasses, and a baseball cap. He had gray hair.

The man looked suspicious. Could he be the tuna fish thief?

He walked up the street. Then he went into Papa's Books!

I took a deep breath and walked into Papa's Books. There, in front of my very eyes, the man was talking to my dad.

My dad said, "Aren't you going to give him a hug? After all, he is your grandpa."

Chapter Five

Okay, sometimes spies make mistakes.

My dad closed the store for lunch. Then we went upstairs with Grandpa.

As we ate, Grandpa explained, "I am an inventor. I like to travel, and I keep all my things in the van. But sometimes I get lonely. So I came here. I would like to stay for a while, if that is all right."

"Of course," said my mom.

There was a shed across the alley. My dad told Grandpa he could keep his inventions in there. Grandpa drove his car into the alley and started to unload things.

There were test tubes. There was a shirt covered with wires and switches. There were little pointy things and big puffy things. There was a toaster with antlers. There were shoes with wings. There were twenty-three computers.

When he finished, I noticed there was one thing still in the van. It was big and lumpy. It was covered with a blanket.

That night, I saw Grandpa in the alley. He opened the back of the van and went inside. He came out pushing a dolly. On the dolly was the big, lumpy thing with a blanket. Grandpa wheeled the dolly into the shed.

Chapter Six

More mysteries!

Why was Grandpa sneaking around at night? What was the big, lumpy thing? Did a toaster really need antlers?

The next morning I wrote down the mysteries in my spy notebook. I read them again and again. I could not think of any answers.

I went to the shed to look around. The windows were covered. A humming noise was coming from inside.

I knocked on the door. No one answered. I went around back where there was an open window. I looked in.

A big chair was in the middle of the room. It sort of looked like something from a rocket ship. And it sort of looked like something from a beauty parlor.

The chair was as big as a throne. There
were wires all over it. There was a helmet
thing sticking up out of the back.

An old, old man sat under the helmet
thing. His face had so many wrinkles that
he probably stayed in the bathtub for
twenty-three years.

There was a blanket on the floor next to
the chair. It was a clue. The chair was the

big, lumpy thing from the van!

The old, old man was wearing overalls and tennis shoes. That was another clue.

The old, old man was Grandpa! But instead of looking sixty years old, he looked ninety years old. Then ninety-one. Then ninety-two.

Grandpa was getting older in front of my eyes!

Chapter Seven

I climbed through the window. I ran over and unplugged the chair.

"I will get help," I told Grandpa.

His voice was like a whisper. "No, please. I will be fine. Just wait one hour. I will get better."

Nothing happened for fifty-nine minutes. At sixty minutes there was a noise. It sounded kind of like when you blow up a balloon.

I looked at Grandpa. His wrinkles were disappearing! His skin was getting pinker. Five minutes later he looked sixty years old again.

He took off his helmet. "Blasted machine!" he said. "It never did work right."

He told me the machine was supposed to

make him younger. But it made him older instead.

"Afterward, do you always get younger again?" I asked.

He nodded. "In exactly one hour you change back to the way you were."

Grandpa pushed the machine into a corner. He covered it with the blanket.

As I watched, I had an idea. Grandpa thought his invention was just a machine that did not work. But when I looked at it, I saw something else.

I saw a way to catch the tuna fish thief.

Chapter Eight

How could the tuna fish thief be caught? Grown-ups.

Grown-ups can do anything. They can stay up past eight o'clock. They can play video games whenever they want. They can talk on the phone for one thousand hours.

If they can do all of these wonderful things, of course they can catch a tuna fish thief. Especially if the grown-up is me.

One day when Grandpa was gone, I sneaked out to the shed. I climbed through the window and went inside.

I took the blanket off the machine. I plugged it in. The humming sound started.

I sat in the chair. I saw a button that said Start and a button that said Stop.

I looked around the room. The next time I saw it, I would be a grown-up.

I reached for the Start button.

"Gotcha!" said a high little voice.

Can you solve the mystery of who was there?

You are right. It was Arthur.

Chapter Nine

Arthur said, "I will tell Grandpa. I will tell Mom and Dad. You will have to stay in your room for the next ninety-seven weeks. Unless . . ."

"Unless what?" I said.

"Unless I can use that machine," he said.

If I agreed, Arthur would find out what the machine did. And he would ruin my genius spy plan. But Grandpa would be getting back soon. I needed to hurry.

"Okay," I said. "But I get the first turn." I took a deep breath. Then I pushed the Start button. The humming sound began.

My clothes were getting tight. I had been wearing a baggy sweatshirt. Only now the sweatshirt wasn't baggy anymore.

I pushed the Stop button. The humming died down.

I got out of the chair. My feet hurt. I looked down. My shoes were smaller.

Then I figured it out. My shoes were not smaller. My feet were bigger!

I took off my shoes and stepped toward Arthur. He backed up.

I looked over and saw a mirror. In the mirror, a strange lady was standing next to Arthur.

Who was the strange lady? My giant spy

brain gave me the answer. It was me!

"Are you Maggie?" squeaked Arthur.

I said, "Of course I am, you little runt."

"Wow," he said, "it really is you."

"We have to hurry," I told Arthur. "Grandpa will be back soon. Get in the chair."

Arthur got in the chair and pushed the Start button. The humming sound began.

I watched the little runt turn into a medium runt, then a big runt. Then all of a sudden he was a grown-up.

I pushed the button. The machine

stopped. Arthur looked down at himself.

"Wow," he said.

It was Arthur speaking. But the voice
sounded like Biff Barksdale, that weather
guy on TV.

"Come on," I said. "We are going to
catch the tuna fish thief. And we only have
one hour to do it."

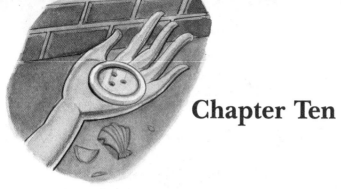

Chapter Ten

We went home and borrowed some of our mom and dad's clothes.

I told Arthur everything. Then I explained my genius spy plan.

I looked at my watch. It showed ten minutes after eleven o'clock.

"Let's hurry," I said. "When twelve o'clock comes, we will turn back into kids."

The first thing we did was check the alley around Mr. Kling's back door. I saw something shiny on the ground.

I picked it up. It was a button. But it was not a regular button. It was big and silver. A clue! There were other shiny things on the ground: little pieces of shell!

"Hey," said Arthur, "I bought a bag of those at the pet store for my goldfish bowl."

"Come on," I said. "We are going to the pet store called Fido's."

We headed for the pet store, doing our best to act like grown-ups.

When we walked in, a voice said, "You are in big trouble."

I whirled around to see who it was. A big green parrot was looking at me.

Ms. Binky stepped out from behind the counter. She ran the pet store.

"Don't mind Petey," she said. "His owner had twelve kids. I guess he heard those words a lot."

I could tell that she didn't recognize us. We had passed our first big test!

I showed her the pieces of shell.

"Did anyone buy a bag of these in the last day or two?" I asked.

Ms. Binky thought for a minute. "Yes, there was a little girl. She got five bags."

"What did she look like?" I asked.

"She had red hair and freckles," said Ms. Binky. "And she was wearing a red dress."

I took the silver button out of my pocket. "Did the dress have buttons like this?"

"I don't know," said Ms. Binky. "But she asked where she could eat. I told her about the restaurant next door called the Hot Spot."

Another clue!

"We're hungry," I said to Arthur. "Right?"

"Not really," he said.

I poked him with my elbow.

"Thank you," I said to Ms. Binky. "Come along, dear."

"You are in big trouble," said Petey.

Chapter Eleven

We were running out of time.

We hurried out of the store and into the Hot Spot.

Arthur found some coins in his pocket and bought a chocolate ice cream cone.

Meanwhile, Miss Brenda came over. She is a waitress and my friend, but that day she didn't recognize me.

"Can I help you, sweetie?" she asked.

Spies hate it when people call them sweetie.

I started to ask her some questions, but there was a problem. When I looked back to check on Arthur, he was not at the counter or at the tables. He was not in the room.

Arthur was gone.

Then I noticed something. There were brown drops on the sidewalk. It was chocolate.

I followed the drops to Shiny Bright Cleaners. Inside, Arthur was standing at the counter, holding the ice cream cone. He had chocolate all over his shirt.

I ran inside. Arthur saw me.

He said, "I spilled ice cream on my shirt. I thought maybe they could clean it."

"In ten minutes?" I asked. I looked at my watch. "Make that five minutes!" I said. "We have to go. Now!"

I pulled Arthur toward the door. Then I noticed something on the floor. It was a silver button.

Chapter Twelve

I bent down to pick up the button. I noticed more buttons. I followed them through a curtain and into a separate room.

There was a man at a sewing machine. Beside him was a girl with red hair.

The girl was working on a cardboard frog. She was pasting silver buttons and shells on it. The most interesting part was the eyes. They were round cans.

The man said, "This is my daughter, Kelsey. She is working on a frog for the contest."

Kelsey said, "We are called Shiny Bright Cleaners. So I thought I would make a shiny bright frog."

"I like the eyes," I said. "What kind of cans are those?"

She said, "Tuna fish."

I said, "I have a friend who lost some cans just like those. He also lost a special plate."

Kelsey started blinking really fast. She went to a cabinet and took out a plate. "Is this it?" she asked.

The plate said Sweetikums.

I heard a sound. It was kind of like a balloon. Suddenly I noticed that Arthur looked different. Like a twenty-six-year-old. Or maybe even a twenty-five-year-old.

"Let's get out of here!" said Arthur.

His voice was squeaky. And his clothes were baggy. We raced outside. We ran and ran. By the time we got to Papa's Books, we had changed back into our usual selves.

We went inside. I shut the door behind us.

"Whew!" I said. "Now we are safe."

I looked up. My dad was standing there. My mom was beside him.

Arthur said, "Uh-oh."

"Uh-oh is right," said my dad. "We are very upset."

My mom said, "The next time you play dress-up with our clothes, you have to ask first. Is that clear?"

I smiled. Our secret was safe. For now.

Saturday was the big frog contest. Arthur and I were there, along with my mom and dad.

Grandpa was there, too. He watched through special glasses that made everything look purple.

"Why do they do that?" I asked.

"I like purple," he said.

There were many great frogs. Mrs.
Levine's frog was totally light bulbs. Mr.
Kling's was Cleopatra. Our frog was covered
with books.

Can you guess which frog won? I will give you a clue. It was the shiniest frog in the contest.

That is right. It was Kelsey's frog from Shiny Bright Cleaners. Keep it up and maybe you will be a spy, too.

Kelsey and her family went up to get the prize. Mr. Kling was behind me, holding Sweetikums.

"Isn't it wonderful?" he said. "Now everything will get back to normal."

I thought of Grandpa and the machine and all the things that had happened. I thought of the many adventures I could

have as a grown-up super genius spy.
Then I smiled.

"No, it won't," I said. "And I don't think it ever will again."